Date Due

MAY 2 9 2001	NOV 1 9 2003
JUN 1 9 2001	DEC 0 3 2003
JUL 0 7 2001	DEC 1 9 2003
	JAN 0 9 2004
MAR 2 8 2002	MAR 2 4 2004
AUG 0 6 2002	OCT 1 4 2004
	OCT 2 6 2004
AUG 1 7 2002	
SEP 1 3 2002	
DEC 1 9 2002	
APR 3 0 2003	
MAY 2 7 2003	
AUG 3 0 2003	

Bungalo Books

To Hayley, Scott, Kristen, Sascha and Jessica
who catch buses every morning without fail

Illustrated by John Bianchi
Written by Frank B. Edwards
Copyright 1995 by Bungalo Books

Canadian Cataloguing in Publication Data

Edwards, Frank B, 1952-
  Mortimer Mooner makes lunch

ISBN 0-921285-37-X (bound)   ISBN 0-921285-36-1 (pbk.)

I. Bianchi, John   II. Title

PS8559.D84M67 1995   jC813'.54   C95-900127-1
PR9199.3.E39 1995

Published in Canada by: Trade Distribution:
Bungalo Books   Firefly Books Ltd.
Ste.100   250 Sparks Avenue
17 Elk Ct.   Willowdale, Ontario
Kingston, Ontario   M2II 2S4
K7M 7A4

Co-published in U.S.A. by: Printed in Canada by:
Firefly Books (U.S.) Inc.   Friesen Printers
Ellicott Station   Altona, Manitoba
P.O. Box 1338   ROG OBO
Buffalo, New York
14205

MORTIMER MOONER MAKES LUNCH

Written by Frank B. Edwards
Illustrated by John Bianchi

BUNGALO BOOKS

It was a bright summer morning when the Mooners slept in. "Jumping Red River Toads, you're late," cried Mortimer Mooner as he pushed his father out of bed. "You have TEN minutes to catch your bus."

Father Mooner raced to the shower. "Mortimer, can you make me a lunch?"

Father Mooner scrubbed his back and washed his hair.
"NINE minutes and counting," called Mortimer as he
got out the bread.

Father Mooner dried himself off and shaved his chin.
"EIGHT minutes to go," reported Mortimer as he
dashed to the refrigerator.

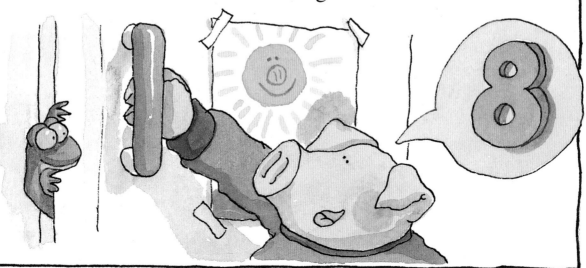

Father Mooner brushed his teeth and combed his hair.

"Only SEVEN minutes remaining," announced Mortimer as he opened the peanut butter jar.

Father Mooner pulled on his socks and hopped
to his closet.

"SIX minutes left," declared Mortimer Mooner.
"Are you dressed yet?" He added some pickles.

Father Mooner jumped into his pants and buttoned up his shirt.

"FIVE minutes," shouted Mortimer as he added some of his father's favourite cheese to the sandwich.

Father Mooner snatched a bright red tie and his very best jacket.

"FOUR…" yelled Mortimer as he crammed the giant sandwich into a plastic bag.

Father Mooner pulled on his shoes and rushed
out of the bedroom.

"THREE..." hollered Mortimer as he grabbed
some fruit and a juice box.

Father Mooner charged down the stairs and headed for the door.

"JUST TWO MINUTES LEFT," screamed Mortimer as he slipped some dessert into his father's briefcase.

"ONE…" thundered Mortimer as he tossed Father Mooner his briefcase and enormous lunch.

"...BLAST OFF!!!!"
Father Mooner caught his lunch and tripped over the morning newspaper. As the lunch and paper flew into the air, he bounced down the steps and landed with a thump!

"Oops, " whispered Mortimer, lifting the paper from his father's face. "I think you're actually kind of early. You don't have to work today after all — it's Saturday. Maybe we can go on a picnic instead!"

"Good idea," groaned Father Mooner, getting to his feet. "But I'm not sure we can eat this huge lunch ourselves."

"Of course, we can…" said Mortimer Mooner.

"...we're pigs!"

The Author and the Illustrator

Frank B. Edwards, a former feature writer and magazine editor, lives with his family near Kingston, Ontario. John Bianchi is a cartoonist, illustrator and author who divides his time between his studio in Arizona's Sonoran Desert, where he lives with his family, and Bungalo World Headquarters.

The pair formed Bungalo Books in 1986 and gave up serious employment shortly after to pursue their love of children's books on a full-time basis.

Official Bungalo Reading Buddies

ONCE UPON A TIME...

Kids who love to read books are eligible to become official, card-carrying Bungalo Reading Buddies. If you and your friends want to join an international club dedicated to having fun while reading, show this notice to your teacher or librarian. We'll send your class a great membership kit. Everyone can become a member.

Teachers and Librarians

Bungalo Books would be pleased to send you a Reading Buddy membership kit that includes 25 full-colour, laminated membership cards. These pocket-sized, 2¼-by-4-inch membership cards can be incorporated into a wide variety of school and community reading programmes for primary, junior and intermediate elementary school students.

* **Each kit includes 25 membership cards, postcards, bookmarks, a current Bungalo Reading Buddy newsletter and a Bungalo storybook.**
* **Kits cost only $7.50 for postage and handling.**
* **No cash please. Make cheque or money order payable to Bungalo Books.**
* **Offer limited to libraries and schools.**
* **Please allow four weeks for delivery.**

SEND TO

Bungalo World Headquarters
Box 129
Newburgh, Ontario
K0K 2S0